但願人長久

千裏共嬋娟

共享一個月亮

To Share One Moon

Story by Ruowen Wang

Illustrated by

Wei Xu & Xiaoyan Zheng

Kevin & Robin Books Ltd.

In loving memory of my adoptive father, Dong Chen Wang,
who has made me what I am today. He is part of my life forever.
— Ruowen Wang

In loving memory of my mother, Wenyu Wang.
— Xiaoyan Zheng

To my dear wife, still in China: The journey of immigration is never easy.
Let's face our future together with courage and hope.
Under the same moon, though thousands of miles apart,
let us think of each other with love, every night.
— Wei Xu

Published 2008 by Kevin & Robin Books Ltd.

Library and Archives Canada Cataloguing in Publication

Wang, Ruowen, 1962–
To share one moon/Ruowen Wang, Wei Xu, Xiaoyan Zheng.

ISBN 978-0-9738799-5-7 (bound)

I. Xu, Wei, 1967– II. Zheng, Xiaoyan, 1957-
III. Title.

PS8645.A534T67 2008   jC813'.6   C2007-904496-4

To Share One Moon
Kevin & Robin Books Ltd.

First Canadian Edition 2008
Printed and bound in Hong Kong, China

 oday is Chinese Mid-Autumn Festival, or Moon Festival. Chinese Moon Festival is very much like Thanksgiving in North America.

On this night, families get together to admire the bright, full moon while eating sweet moon cakes and enjoying a cup of good tea. Under this full moon friendships are renewed, families are reunited, and long-lost loved ones find their way to each other. Under the bright moonlight people toast each other's good health, family togetherness, and wish peace for everyone. It is a time to reflect, to think of our absent loved ones, and to wish our families and friends well.

Two years ago, my family celebrated our last Moon Festival in China before moving to Canada. Many relatives and friends came to our farewell party. Our two maids cooked from morning till night. Mama bought dozens of moon cakes.

Papa was a doctor, and Mama held a high-ranking position in a large bank. We had a comfortable life. People could not understand why we would give up everything and move to Canada. Papa said it was for me to receive a better education. Mama joked that the moon in Canada was fuller and brighter than the one in China. I was puzzled: Don't we all have just one moon?

I cried for days, because my old nanny who had raised me since I was born could not come along and had to return to her home in a poor village.

The night before my nanny's departure, she pointed at the full Mid-Autumn moon and told me, "Niu Niu (which is Chinese Mandarin for 'girl'), just look at that big, round moon. The full moon symbolizes unity. An ancient poet once pointed out that we are all under the same moon, even though thousands of miles apart. Tonight, all loved ones are thinking of each other, no matter how far apart they are. I want you to remember that I will always be thinking of you."

My family — Mama, Papa, Nai Nai (Papa's mama) and I landed in Toronto. Papa's older brother, Uncle Lin, picked us up at the airport. We would stay at his house until we could find a place of our own.

Uncle Lin came to Canada fifteen years ago. He loves Canada very much. For the first few days, Uncle Lin took us around and showed us many wonderful sights. He took care to point out everything he was proud of: Government officials were humble and courteous. Libraries and schools were free. Children of many races played happily together. People were well mannered. The streets were clean. The traffic was orderly. Even the police were kind, friendly and helpful.

My parents were very happy. They said they had found heaven on earth. With excitement and hope, we looked forward to our new lives in Canada.

Uncle Lin suggested that in order to save money, we rent a small two-bedroom basement apartment for the time being. Nai Nai and I would share the smaller bedroom.

Papa said, "We will buy a large house after I find a good job. It won't be long."

But Uncle Lin said, "It may take longer than you think."

It was Mid-Autumn Festival again, our first
Chinese Moon Festival in Canada. The full moon
was hanging over the east horizon. It was
extremely large and bright. So beautiful, and so
close by, it made me want to cry because I missed
my nanny.

Nai Nai was homesick too. She missed all our relatives and
friends in China. I told Nai Nai about the ancient poet and his
words. Nai Nai in turn told me an old Chinese story about the Moon
Lady — Chang-Er.

"*O*nce upon a time, there were ten suns taking turns circling around the earth.

"One day, the ten suns decided to be mischievous, and they all showed up at once. The earth became as hot as an oven, the crops started to wither up, and the livestock were dying of thirst.

"People turned to the Queen Mother of the West, the wife of the almighty Chinese God, for help.

"The Queen Mother of the West sent for Hou Yi, a mighty archer. With his magic arrows, Hou Yi shot nine suns down and left one to keep the earth bright and comfortably warm.

"To reward Hou Yi's bravery and skill, the Queen Mother of the West let him pick one of her prettiest maids to take home as his wife, and also gave him two pearls — the pearls of everlasting life. She told him, 'Wait for the Mid-Autumn moon to turn full. Then swallow one of the pearls, and you will live forever. Swallow two, and you will fly to heaven and live *happily* forever.'

"Hou Yi planned to share the pearls with his beloved wife, Chang-Er. When they got home, he gave the pearls to her for safekeeping until the moon grew full again.

"But then, the Queen Mother of the West called on Hou Yi for another mission. While he was away from home, the moon kept growing fuller and fuller.

"Finally, Chang-Er could not bear to wait any longer. She took out the pearls and swallowed one. Right away, she felt younger and more beautiful. Even her body felt lighter. Chang-Er was delighted. The thought of living in heaven *happily forever* was so tempting that she popped the second pearl into her mouth.

"Immediately, Chang-Er found herself floating. Fearing that she would be lonely in heaven, Chang-Er grabbed her white rabbit to take with her as she flew out the window and into the sky.

"The Queen Mother of the West was ashamed of her former maid's selfishness. To punish Chang-Er, the Queen Mother of the West waved her silk fan. Its wind blew Chang-Er away and kept her far from heaven's door.

"Chang-Er flew and flew, until finally she landed on the cold moon. There, she lived alone in regret, with only her white rabbit for company.

"Chang-Er wanted very much to return to earth and her husband. So she picked some white cassia flowers, and gave a pestle and a mortar to the rabbit to pound them into a pearl-like homecoming pill."

Nai Nai pointed at the bright moon and said, "Tonight, if you look up at the moon when it is full, you can still see Chang-Er, her long gown floating in the wind and, by her side, the white rabbit pounding away."

It was a sad story. I prefer stories with happy endings. Poor Chang-Er. I looked up at the moon. I could vaguely see a figure, and another white spot that could be the rabbit. As I stared up at the moon, I could almost see the figure moving. Will the Moon Lady ever get to come down from the moon? I wished she could return home to her husband. Or better still, that she had never left him in the first place.

The moon in Canada is fuller and brighter than the one in China, after all. Papa said it was because of the cleaner air. This time, Mama did not make another joke about it.

Our first Chinese Moon Festival in Canada was quiet. There were no relatives or friends around to share it with and no family celebrations. We were all too busy working and studying to even remember this traditional occasion.

Only Nai Nai did not forget. Nai Nai reminded Mama to buy some moon cakes.

To Nai Nai's dismay, though, Mama bought only two moon cakes for the four of us to share.

"Moon cakes in Canada are too sweet," Mama explained.

"Or too expensive," said Nai Nai under her breath, to point out the truth behind Mama's excuse.

The money we had brought with us was about to run out. Mama could not find a high-ranking position in a bank. She went back to school to improve her English. Papa, even though he spoke good English, could not be a doctor again because he had not been trained in Canada. To keep our family fed, he had to take a job in a small factory, making muffins.

Uncle Lin said it was a "labour" job. The word *labour* sounds very close to the Mandarin words *lei boer*, meaning "to tire the neck."

Nai Nai was unhappy. "Can't you find a job that does not *lei boer*? You are not fit for physical work. Why do you have to work in a factory and make *ma fan*?" (In Mandarin, *ma fan* means "trouble.")

Nai Nai's mix-up made Papa and me laugh, but Mama weep. Mama went into her room and shut the door.

Another year in Canada has slipped away. Many things have happened. Nai Nai did not like living in a basement, so we rented a small house. Mama went back to China to her high-ranking position, shortly after the last Mid-Autumn Festival.

Nai Nai became sick and stayed in a hospital for two weeks. She was deeply touched by her experience.

"Canadian doctors and nurses took good care of me, just like my own sons and daughters," she exclaimed and told Papa, "When you become a Canadian doctor, you will have to be like that."

Papa started to volunteer in a hospital on weekends and attend school at night. He was determined to become a doctor again, in Canada.

We all missed Mama and hoped she would return to us soon.

Our house seems empty and lacking warmth without Mama.

The weather is cool. The air is crisp and fresh. Tonight, the moon seems even fuller and brighter than our first Canadian Mid-Autumn moon. But Papa and Nai Nai do not seem to notice it. I do not want to mention anything either, for fear of stirring up sad feelings.

Papa has bought two moon cakes. Nai Nai can only eat a little, and shares one with me.

"Canadian moon cakes are too sweet," Nai Nai says. I know she is thinking of Mama.

Papa eats half of his moon cake quietly, and then puts the other half away.

At night, while Papa and Nai Nai are asleep, I sit by the window looking up at the bright, full moon. I am thinking of Mama and my nanny, and wondering if they are looking up now and sharing the same moon with me. The ancient poet and his words occur to me again, which also reminds me of Nai Nai's story about the Moon Lady, Chang-Er.

A small piece of passing cloud wafts across the moon. Is the figure in the moon moving? I'm sure it is. I imagine the Moon Lady floating down from the moon, drifting right through my open window, and suddenly changing into Mama.

"Have you eaten up my share of the moon cake, too?" she'd ask.

Aha, maybe that is why Papa has saved the other half of his moon cake!

I miss Mama very much, especially tonight. I wonder if she will ever come back to us. She must be very lonely now. Does she know of the ancient Chinese poet and his words? Has Nai Nai ever told Mama the story of Chang-Er? Does Mama miss us tonight?

Under the bright Mid-Autumn moon, I make three wishes and believe they will be granted: I wish that this full moon has the magic power to hold families together. I wish that the Moon Lady will eventually return to her husband, who is still awaiting her on earth. And I wish that all loved ones, no matter where they are, will look up at this full moon tonight and think of each other with a tender heart.